PINK
IS for
EVERYBODY!

PINK IS for EVERYBODY!

Written by Ella Russell
Illustrated by Udayana Lugo

Owlkids Books

Gray is for rainy days.

But what is pink for?

It's for all *kinds* of bows, from the top of your head all the way down to the looping laces of your shoes.

Pink is for the buttons
lining your front.
It's for a checkered shirt,
a poofy skirt,
and a pair of fuzzy socks.
(That's pink times two!)

But there are those who
find pink puzzling.
They sometimes even wonder …
Who is pink for?

Pink is for painters, of course!
It's for partygoers … and even party poopers.
It's for palace dwellers, if you please.

And who else is it for?

Pink is for astronauts! And aliens.
Dancers and dragons.

Circus folk, tightrope walkers,
firefighters, and cow herders.
(Yeehaw!)

That includes pilots and pirates
and all sorts of swashbucklers.
It's even for lions and tigers
and bears, oh—

WAIT!

Pink is not for *everybody*.

Pink is most definitely,
ab-so-tootly, cer-ter-tainly
not for ...

... anybody who doesn't like pink!

Much better.

But who are bow ties for?

Cats, of course!

(Or anybody who
likes to wear one.)

For everybody who loves pink, and anybody who doesn't.
But most of all, for Théo —E.R.

To my parents, who always let me play with all the colors —U.L.

Text © 2022 Ella Russell
Illustrations © 2022 Udayana Lugo

Owlkids Books acknowledges the financial support of the Canada Council for the Arts, the Ontario Arts Council, the Government of Canada through the Canada Book Fund (CBF) and the Government of Ontario through the Ontario Creates Book Initiative for our publishing activities.

Published in Canada by
Owlkids Books Inc.
1 Eglinton Avenue East
Toronto, ON M4P 3A1

Published in the United States by
Owlkids Books Inc.
1700 Fourth Street
Berkeley, CA 94710

Library and Archives Canada Cataloguing in Publication

Title: Pink Is for everybody / written by Ella Russell ; illustrated by Udayana Lugo.
Names: Russell, Ella, author. | Lugo, Udayana, illustrator.
Identifiers: Canadiana 1258124722 | ISBN 9781771474658 (hardcover)
Classification: LCC PS8635.U869 P56 2022 | DDC jC813/.6—dc23

Library of Congress Control Number: 2021942224

Edited by Stacey Roderick
Designed by Claudia Dávila

Manufactured in Shenzhen, Guangdong, China, in October 2021, by C & C Offset
Job #HV4343

A   B   C   D   E   F

ONTARIO ARTS COUNCIL
CONSEIL DES ARTS DE L'ONTARIO
an Ontario government agency
un organisme du gouvernement de l'Ontario

Canada Council
for the Arts

Conseil des Arts
du Canada

Canada

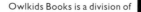

Owl kids
Publisher of Chirp, Chickadee and OWL
www.owlkidsbooks.com

Owlkids Books is a division of bayard canada